Magic Kitten

A Summer Spell

Bradley—my lovely, laid-back blue boy.

GROSSET & DUNLAP
Published by the Penguin Group
Penguin Group (USA) Inc., 375 Hudson Street, New York, New York 10014,
USA
Penguin Group (Canada), 90 Eglinton Avenue East, Suite 700, Toronto, Ontario
M4P 2Y3, Canada
(a division of Pearson Penguin Canada Inc.)
Penguin Books Ltd., 80 Strand, London WC2R 0RL, England
Penguin Group Ireland, 25 St. Stephen's Green, Dublin 2, Ireland
(a division of Penguin Books Ltd.)
Penguin Group (Australia), 250 Camberwell Road, Camberwell, Victoria 3124,
Australia
(a division of Pearson Australia Group Pty. Ltd.)
Penguin Books India Pvt. Ltd., 11 Community Centre, Panchsheel Park,
New Delhi—110 017, India
Penguin Group (NZ), 67 Apollo Drive, Rosedale, North Shore 0632, New Zealand
(a division of Pearson New Zealand Ltd.)
Penguin Books (South Africa) (Pty.) Ltd., 24 Sturdee Avenue,
Rosebank, Johannesburg 2196, South Africa

Penguin Books Ltd., Registered Offices:
80 Strand, London WC2R 0RL, England

Text copyright © 2006 Sue Bentley. Illustrations copyright © 2006 Angela Swan.
Cover illustration copyright © 2006 Andrew Farley. First printed in Great Britain in
2006 by Penguin Books Ltd. First published in the United States in 2008 by Grosset
& Dunlap, a division of Penguin Young Readers Group, 345 Hudson Street, New
York, New York 10014. GROSSET & DUNLAP is a trademark of Penguin Group
(USA) Inc. Printed in the U.S.A.

Library of Congress Cataloging-in-Publication Data is available.

ISBN 978-0-448-44998-2   30 29 28 27 26 25 24 23

Magic Kitten

A Summer Spell

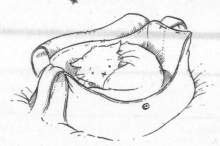

SUE BENTLEY

Illustrated by Angela Swan

Grosset & Dunlap

Prologue

A flash of bright white light crossed the sky. A shower of silver sparkles fell upon a young white lion. Before the lion had a chance to blink, it was magically changed into a tiny, fluffy, orange kitten.

Just then, an old gray lion ran up to the little orange kitten and bowed his head. "Prince Flame! You have transformed yourself perfectly! Your Uncle Ebony will never recognize you now. But you must hurry. He is on his way to find you. If he catches you, he will kill you. He will stop at nothing until he has your throne for himself."

"Cirrus, my friend. Save yourself!"
Prince Flame meowed, his emerald eyes
flashing. "I will face him."

"Please, Flame. You must stay
disguised as a kitten and hide until you
are strong enough to fight your uncle on
your own."

Flame shivered. "Where should I hide?
My kingdom is no longer safe for me.
Uncle Ebony's spies are everywhere . . ."

Cirrus laid a paw on the young
prince's little orange head. "Go far away.
Grow strong and wise. Return when
you are ready to claim the Lion Throne
for yourself and rid the land of your evil
uncle."

Flame gasped as an enormous adult

lion appeared out of nowhere and lunged toward them. The lion's teeth were bared.

Silver sparks ignited in Flame's fur and the kitten meowed as he felt the magic and power building inside him.

The older lion growled and showed his teeth. And just as he leaped onto a flat rock near Flame and Cirrus, there was a bright blue flash of light. Flame heard the lion roar, then felt himself falling. The magic had worked. He was safe for now.

Chapter
ONE

Lisa Morgan gave a sigh as the train
drew to a halt. Long Brackby Station
had no waiting room. There was just a
wooden platform and some steps that led
down to the road. She was surrounded by
miles of open countryside.

"Great, I'm being dumped in the
middle of nowhere," she grumbled.
"Thanks a lot, Mom and Dad!"

Her parents had gone to America on
business. But Lisa was going to stay with
her Aunt Rose, who she hadn't seen
since she was a baby.

Lisa scanned the platform. She saw a woman with braids and flowing clothes hurrying toward her. Her heart sank. Aunt Rose was an old hippie!

I bet she has weird ideas about food, Lisa thought glumly. She imagined being force-fed beans, lettuce, and raw carrots. She pictured herself looking all limp and pale. That would serve her parents right!

The hippie woman smiled. She dashed straight past Lisa and jumped on the train.

"Phew!" Lisa breathed, feeling relieved but a bit disappointed. She had actually liked the idea of making her parents feel guilty for not taking her with them.

Just then a voice called out, "Hi, Lisa! I'm over here!"

A thin woman with wavy brown hair was climbing the platform steps. She wore jeans and a yellow T-shirt. She waved at Lisa.

Lisa waved back.

"Sorry I'm late." Rose gathered Lisa up and gave her a big hug. She then held Lisa at arm's length and studied her. "Gosh, aren't you tall for ten years old?"

"Everyone says that," Lisa murmured.

"Dad says I take after him."

"I think you're right." Rose's smile was warm. It made her eyes twinkle. "It's so nice to have you here for the school vacation. We can really get to know each other."

Lisa felt a little better after Rose's warm welcome. But she wasn't ready to let go of her bad mood. "I didn't want to come here. Mom forced me to stay with you."

Rose looked amused. She picked up Lisa's suitcase. "Well—I'd better make sure you enjoy yourself! Long Brackby may not compare with America, but it has a lot to offer. Come on. Let's go home. The car's this way."

Lisa followed her aunt down the steps. The garage was empty. "Did someone steal your car?" she asked worriedly.

"Oh, no. Matilda's over there." Rose pointed across a wide field. "She conked out on me, I'm afraid. That's why I was late."

Lisa craned her neck. She could just see the rounded top of a red car above a hedge. It looked about a hundred miles away!

Rose grinned at Lisa's expression. "It's only a short walk. I'm sure you wouldn't mind stretching your legs after two hours on the train." She opened a big wooden gate and stepped into the field.

Lisa hung back nervously. There were lots of enormous black-and-white cows in the field. "Won't they chase us?" she asked.

"Not if we don't chase them," Rose

joked. "Just follow me. You'll be fine." She closed the gate behind them and set off.

After a couple of feet, Rose stopped suddenly. "Oh, look, how pretty. That's ragged robin . . ." She pointed to a clump of pink wildflowers.

"Oh." Lisa almost bumped into her aunt. She was keeping a wary eye on the cows. One of them, which seemed about the size of a bus, was staring hard at her. She was sure it was going to charge at any moment. Rose set off again. "Lisa, you'd better watch out for the . . ." she began.

Lisa's foot sank right into something soft and smelly. She skidded and almost slipped over. "Ugh! How gross is that!"

". . . cow pies," Rose finished.

"My sneakers!" Lisa wailed. "They're ruined."

Rose's mouth twitched. "Oh, well, it's only a bit of old poo. We can hose it off when we get home. Good thing you didn't slip and fall in it!"

Lisa scowled at Rose. "Ha, ha," she muttered angrily.

Peering down at her sneaker, Lisa hopped on one foot, trying to wipe the sole clean on the grass. When she looked up again, she saw that Rose was almost at the other end of the field.

"Wait for me!" she shouted in panic. She raced across the field and shot through the gate. There was no way she was going to be left behind with the cows, to be trampled into a human pancake!

Rose walked along until she came to her car. "Here we are. Say hello to Matilda."

Rose's VW Beetle was painted black and tomato red. It looked like a giant, rather battered, ladybug.

"Oh—my—goodness," Lisa mouthed silently. "Will that old thing start?"

"*She*, please," Rose corrected.

"Matilda always starts after a rest." She
opened the hood, which Lisa saw was
actually the trunk, and put Lisa's suitcase
inside. When they were both seated,
Rose started the engine. "Hurrah! First
time!" she cried.

Despite herself, Lisa smiled.

A couple of minutes later, they
drove up to a neat thatched cottage.
White roses scrambled all over the
honey-colored stone walls.

"Leave your sneakers on the front
step. You can clean them later," Rose
said. "Would you like a cold drink?"
Rose asked.

"Yes, please." Lisa followed her aunt
through to the kitchen. A big teapot sat
on top of Rose's stove. There was also a

deep sink and a wooden dresser, but no dishwasher, toaster, or microwave.

"Now, what can I get you?" asked Rose.

"A Coke, please," Lisa said.

Rose frowned. "I'm afraid I've only got lemonade. It's homemade. Would you like to try it?"

Lisa wrinkled her nose, but she was dying of thirst so she accepted a glass. She took a tiny sip. It wasn't as bad as she'd expected.

"Come on. I'll give you the grand tour." Rose led the way into a room filled with afternoon sunshine.

Lisa saw a sofa with big patchwork cushions and lots of bookcases. "Through there is my workroom." Rose pointed toward an open door.

Lisa peered inside. There were shelves piled with folded material, and glass jars crammed with colorful beads and buttons. "I thought Mom said you were an artist."

Rose chuckled. "I'm a textile artist. I make patchwork quilts and wall hangings."

"Oh," Lisa said. That sounded really boring. "What's upstairs?"

Rose explained that there were two bedrooms. One was hers and Lisa would be using the other.

"It's a little small, isn't it?" Lisa said. She was sure Rose's entire cottage would fit into the living room of her parents' apartment in London.

"I like to think of it as cozy," said Rose with a smile. "It suits me just fine. Why don't we sit down and finish our drinks before I show you your room?"

"Okay," Lisa shrugged. She plonked herself down on Rose's squishy sofa. Something didn't seem quite right with the room. Then, with a shock, she realized why. "You don't have a TV!"

"Oh, I don't bother with watching the box. I always have so much to do," Rose said.

Lisa was speechless. She didn't know *anyone* who didn't have a TV.

Rose took one look at Lisa's glum face. She chuckled. "I've got an old set in the closet. I'll get it for you, if you like."

Lisa shrugged. "I don't mind."

Five minutes later, Rose came in carrying a small black-and-white TV. "Here you go."

Lisa just stared. "It's only got four channels!"

Rose frowned. "How many should it have?"

"I don't know. But ours at home has at least thirty."

"Really?" Rose looked astonished.

"However do they fill that many channels? Well, if you don't want it . . ."

"No, I do. I do!" Lisa decided quickly.

She watched as Rose set about plugging in the TV. No microwave and a TV that should be in a museum. This vacation was going to be a nightmare.

Chapter
TWO

As Lisa finished stuffing her clothes into a drawer, her aunt called up the stairs.

"Lisa! Why don't you have a look around outside while I'm cooking dinner? There's something that might interest you in the barn."

Lisa padded downstairs in her socks. Rose was in the kitchen by the back door. She gave Lisa some green rain boots. "You can borrow these."

Lisa rolled her eyes. "Oh, good!" she murmured.

Rose chuckled. "They might not be the height of fashion, but they'll keep your feet clean!"

Rose's garden had a long narrow lawn and a big vegetable plot. The old barn was right at the bottom. Lisa wandered down to it. She hoped the barn wasn't dark and creepy and full of horrible spiders.

Just as she opened the door there was a bright silver flash. Lisa thought she saw a large white shape out of the corner of her eye. She turned her head, but saw only a pile of old newspapers.

She pushed the door wide open and poked her head in. A warm, slightly musty smell greeted her. It was somehow familiar. Lisa went right inside. She could see rows of cages and pens. Now she

recognized that smell. It was just like inside a pet shop.

"Look at all these animals! This is great!" There were rabbits, guinea pigs, and even some hedgehogs. "Aunt Rose must be into animal rescue."

Sacks of animal food were stored on a bench. Lisa noticed a glow coming from one of the food sacks. "That's strange." She went over to investigate.

"Oh!" She gazed in amazement.

A fluffy orange-colored kitten was curled up on one of the sacks. Silver sparkles glittered in the air around it and its whiskers crackled like electricity.

Lisa stared and stared at the kitten. It looked so real. Was it some kind of new toy? No cat in the world sparkled like that.

Suddenly the kitten's eyes shot open. It took one look at Lisa and hurtled into the air on stiff little legs. "Meow! Monster!" it cried fearfully.

"Argh!" Lisa yelled in shock. Did this kitten really just speak?

Lisa took a step back, fell over her own feet, and landed on her bottom in the straw.

The kitten gazed at her with glowing

emerald eyes. Its fur all stood on end. Silver sparkles crackled all round it. "What are you?" it demanded in a velvety meow.

"I'm a girl," Lisa stammered in complete shock. "What are you?"

But the kitten didn't seem to hear her. "A girl?" it repeated to itself. "Strange. You have two legs. No tail or whiskers."

"Of course I don't! I'm not a cat!" Lisa said. She rose to her feet slowly, so that the amazing kitten wouldn't run away. "My name's Lisa Morgan."

"Lisa," the kitten meowed, looking up at her. It seemed strangely unafraid of her, despite how tiny it was. "Where is this place, Lisa?"

"It's a village called Long Brackby," she replied. "My aunt Rose lives here.

I'm staying with her for vacation. What are you doing here? Who are you? *What* are you?"

"I am Prince Flame," replied the kitten, sitting up very straight. "Heir to the Lion Throne."

"Wow! Really?" Lisa was having trouble taking everything in. A royal cat. A magic, talking cat. Here, in her aunt's barn! Lisa thought for a moment. She was confused. "Did you say *Lion* Throne? But you're only a kit—" She was suddenly interrupted as Flame pricked up his ears.

"What is that big noise?"

Lisa heard a car go by on the road outside. "Just a car. It's okay. It won't hurt you." She had a sudden thought. "Are you hungry? Aunt Rose must have loads of cat food. I can get you some if you like."

Lisa saw Flame's eyes light up at the thought of food. "You are kind, Lisa. This is a safe place."

He leaped forward. There was a

bright blue flash and a crackle of silver sparks.

"Oh!" Lisa was blinded for a second. When her sight cleared, she saw that in Flame's place stood a young, regal, white lion. Then just as suddenly as it had appeared, Flame returned as the fluffy orange kitten.

"Flame? Was that you?" she gasped. "You really are a lion prince!"

Flame blinked up at her with wide, emerald-green eyes. "I am in danger. I must hide. Will you keep me safe?" he asked in a tiny meow.

Lisa's heart melted. Flame was impressive as a royal lion. Disguised as a kitten he was adorable. "Oh, of course I will!" Picking him up, she gently pet the top of his head. Then she paused for a moment. "But what are you hiding from?"

Flame placed his tiny paws on Lisa's chest and looked up at her. "My uncle wants my throne. His spies seek me here. He wants—he wants to kill me."

"Well, they'll have to fight me first!" Lisa said fiercely. "I'll look after you,

Flame," she promised. "You'll be my secret. My secret magic kitten. Although I don't know what I'm going to tell Aunt Rose. She's going to notice you if you live here."

"Notice who?" asked a voice at her side. "Who are you talking to, Lisa?"

Lisa almost jumped out of her skin. She hadn't heard Aunt Rose come into the barn.

Chapter
THREE

"I found Flame asleep on a sack of food. Please can I keep him?" Lisa asked, stroking Flame's tiny ears.

"Flame? I see you've already given him a name." Rose pet the kitten's soft orange fur. "He's beautiful all right. But we should find out where he lives. He's not one of the rescued animals, you know."

"He doesn't have a home or he wouldn't be sleeping in a barn, would he?" Lisa reasoned. She had promised Flame she would take care of him and

there was *no way* she was letting him
down. "If you let Flame live here, I'll
do everything for him. I'll buy his food
with my allowance. He can sleep in my
bedroom. And . . . and . . . I'll clean out
stinky animal cages and everything!"

Rose laughed. "You're determined to
keep him, aren't you?"

"Completely!" Lisa said excitedly.
"So—can he stay?"

"You should give him to me then,"
Rose said. "I'll check him for fleas and
ticks before he comes into the house."

"Stupendous! You can stay here.
We're going to be best friends," Lisa
whispered, giving Flame a quick hug
before handing him to her aunt.

"Hello there, you sweet thing." Rose
ran expert fingers through Flame's soft
coat. "No flea dirt showing, so far."
She then turned him over and searched
the paler fur on his fat, round tummy.
"Good, none there either."

Flame wriggled and meowed in
protest.

Lisa had to bite back a grin. She
suspected this was the first time a lion

prince had been searched for fleas!

Rose finished her examination. "He's clean and in very good condition. I'm sure he's hungry. You'll find food and a feeding dish on that shelf."

"Thanks, Aunt Rose! You're wonderful!" Lisa hugged her aunt on impulse.

Rose gave her a pleased smile. "Anyone would think you'd never had a pet!"

"I haven't. Mom says it isn't fair to have animals in an apartment." Lisa opened a can, forked food into a dish, and set it on the floor.

Flame purred loudly as he munched on the cat food.

"Well, I agree with your mom about pets," Rose said seriously. "Don't get too attached to Flame. You'll have a tough decision to make when you go back to London."

Lisa knew that Rose was right. But it was too late. She had promised Flame she would look after him, and this magic kitten was the one good thing that had happened since her parents had left her here. She didn't want to give him up!

Flame licked his lips when he'd finished the food. He came and rubbed his body against Lisa's legs. She bent down to pet him and he meowed softly, so only she heard him.

"I am safe with you. Thank you, Lisa."

Rose dug a scoop into a sack of rabbit food.

"I'll help." This wasn't exactly Lisa's idea of fun, but she was determined to show that she meant to keep her promise and make certain that Flame could stay.

For the next half-hour she refilled water bottles, chopped vegetables, and replaced soiled straw.

Flame settled down, tucked his paws

beneath his body, and dozed.

"Thanks, love," Rose said later as she and Lisa washed their hands. "I bet you're ready to eat. I know I am."

Lisa scooped up the sleepy kitten and followed Rose back to the cottage. Rose gave her an old blanket and Lisa spread it on the sofa. Flame jumped straight up and began pedaling it into a soft nest with his front paws.

A few minutes later, Rose brought heaping plates of food to the table.

"Er . . . thanks." Lisa poked the food with her knife. It was shepherd's pie with a lot of fresh green stuff next to it.

"That's called salad. We eat a lot of it in the country. It's the law!" Rose kept a straight face.

"I get the message," Lisa said with

a grin. The pie was delicious and she
even ate some of the salad. Afterward,
Lisa went to sit near Flame on the sofa.
"Thanks, Aunt Rose. I think I'll curl up
with Flame and watch TV now."

"Do you mind doing that later?" Rose

said. "House rules are—I cook, you wash up. Okay?"

"Oh, right." Lisa felt herself blush. She jumped up and collected the dishes. Wasn't there even a dishwasher here?

In the kitchen, Lisa filled the sink with hot water and squirted dish-washing liquid over the pots and pans. As she began scrubbing them clean, suds foamed up past her elbows. "Uh-oh," she said worriedly as more suds waterfalled onto the kitchen floor and slopped around her feet. "I think I overdid it! What a mess. Aunt Rose is going to kill me!"

"May I help?" came a tiny voice from the kitchen floor.

She turned to see that Flame stood behind her. His orange fur was fizzing with huge silver sparkles, his whiskers crackled, and his eyes glowed like emerald coals. Lisa felt a hot prickling sensation down her spine.

Something was about to happen!

Chapter
FOUR

Flame leaped up into the air like a silver fireball and landed on the draining board. Sparks crackled from the tips of his ears.

He waved his front paws, and plates, spoons, forks, knives, and pans all dunked themselves in the suds. One by one, they jumped into the air, and spun themselves dry.

Lisa's eyes widened. "Wow! This is *so* cool!"

Cabinet doors flew open and clean plates stacked themselves on the shelves. Drawers opened, so that forks, knives, and spoons could zoom inside.

Lisa watched the suds drain away. The dishcloth did a little dance as it wiped the sink clean. Another cloth shimmied across the kitchen floor. "Look at them go!" She clapped her hands with delight.

"Lisa? Are you all right? There's a lot

of noise in there," Rose called from the living room.

"Oh, no!" Lisa's hand flew to her mouth. She waved frantically at Flame. "Quick. Stop doing whatever you're doing!" she hissed. "I'm fine. Almost finished!" she called to her aunt, in what she hoped was a normal voice.

Crash! Cabinet doors closed. *Bang!* Drawers slammed shut. *Rattle!* Silverware settled into place.

Seconds later, Rose popped her head around the kitchen door. "What *is* going on in here?"

Flame sat on the floor, looking just like a normal orange kitten. Phew! Lisa let out her breath and gave her aunt a rather shaky smile. That was a close call!

"I'm really impressed. The whole

kitchen's spotless. Well done," Rose said admiringly.

"Oh, it was nothing," Lisa said, shining the back of her nails on her T-shirt.

She winked at Flame, who gave a mischievous "meow."

A big bubble of laughter lodged in Lisa's chest. With Flame around, she reckoned this vacation might not be so bad after all.

The following morning, Lisa woke up early. She lay with her eyes closed, listening for the sound of traffic and taxi horns honking in impatience. But only birdsong drifted in on the fresh breeze from the open window. Lisa opened her eyes as she remembered where she was.

Aunt Rose's cottage in Long Brackby. And yesterday she had found a magic kitten in the barn! Now he was curled up asleep with her.

Flame purred softly in his sleep. As Lisa pet him gently, Flame stretched and yawned, showing his little pink tongue and sharp white teeth. Silver sparks glittered in his fur.

"I slept well, thank you," he purred
happily.

"Me too," Lisa said as Flame rubbed
his head under her chin. "That tickles!"
she said with a grin. She pulled herself
up out of bed and went in search of the
bathroom as Flame made himself comfy
on her pillow and waited.

Rose was already in the kitchen when
Lisa came down. Lisa fed Flame before
she ate her breakfast and then helped
Rose clear up, smiling as she remembered
how the dishes got cleaned yesterday!

"Do you want to bike to the village
store?" Rose asked. "We need milk,
bread, and eggs, but I've got tons of
sewing to do," she explained. "You
could use my bike. It would help me

out and would give you a chance to explore."

"Sounds great," Lisa said. Having Flame along would make even boring old shopping fun!

Rose fetched her bike. It had a deep basket on the front. Lisa lined it with Flame's blanket and then lifted him in.

"There. It's just right for you!"

Flame purred softly in agreement.

Rose laughed. "You know, I think that kitten understands every word you say!"

She came around to the front of the cottage to give Lisa directions to the village shops. "Go up Berry Road to the crossroads and turn right. You'll see the White Hart Inn. The shops are just a bit farther on. You can't miss them."

Rose's red and black VW Beetle was parked by the gate. "Hi, Matilda!" Lisa called as she cycled past. "See you later, Aunt Rose!"

The honey scent of hawthorn filled the lane. Skylarks circled overhead, drifting on the warm air. Flame had his nose in the air, sniffing the delicious country smells.

"Now—we turn here," Lisa reminded herself.

Berry Road was narrow and lined with trees. Lisa began to slow down as she approached a sharp bend.

Suddenly a brown and white pony came hurtling toward her. Lisa caught a glimpse of the rider pulling at the reins. The pony's ears were flat against its head. It snorted loudly, flaring its nostrils.

"Watch out!" shouted the rider. "I can't stop him!"

Lisa squeezed the brakes hard so that pebbles sprayed the grass shoulder. Flame dug his claws into the basket to brace himself.

But it was too late. They were going to crash!

Chapter
FIVE

Lisa's bike screeched along the road into the pony. The brakes locked and she was launched into the air. Just as she prepared herself for a very painful landing, there was a silver flash and she landed softly onto what felt like a very soft pillow.

"Oh!" she cried in surprise. She pushed herself shakily to her feet and looked down, but there was just the grass beneath her. That was a close call. Flame must have used his magic to save her! But where was he?

Lisa looked around in panic. In the road she saw the pony was snorting with pain and fear. His rider was trying to calm him down. Aunt Rose's bike lay on its side in the road, the pedals still going around. Flame's crumpled blanket was lying beside it.

Lisa's heart lurched. "Oh, no! Flame!"

But Flame was sitting in the gutter, calmly washing his face. He gave a pleased little meow as she bent down to pet him.

"Oh, thank goodness you're okay!" Lisa said.

"Yeah? Well, Fly's not. And it's all your fault!" shouted the boy who'd been riding the pony. "Why don't you look where you're going?"

Stung, Lisa glared at him. The boy looked about twelve. He had dark brown hair and bright blue eyes. "You were on the wrong side of the road!" she protested angrily, picking up her bike.

But the boy ignored her. "Whoa, there. Calm down, Fly!" he soothed. The pony rolled his eyes and kept lifting one back leg. "Oh, great. Now he's lame! Dad's going to kill me. We don't have any money for vet's bills."

Lisa felt sorry for the pony, but she was still furious with its owner. "You should be more careful how you ride him then! Look at my aunt's bike. The front wheel's all bent!"

Flame finished washing himself. He padded over to Fly. Lisa started forward in alarm. Did Flame realize what danger he was in?

"Get that kitten out of the way. Fly's scared of other animals," the boy warned.

Flame stopped right beneath Fly. He looked straight up at the pony, his emerald eyes sparkling. Fly shifted sideways and gave a nervous blow. Then he dipped his head. Flame purred loudly, closing his eyes with pleasure as Fly snuffed warm breath into his fur.

The boy scratched his head. "Will you

look at that? Fly's really taken to that kitten." He ran a hand down his pony's sore leg. "And his leg seems better now. How did that happen?"

Lisa smiled inwardly as she bent down and picked Flame up. "Thanks for saving me. And making Fly's leg better," she whispered.

"I am glad to help." Flame licked her chin with his tiny pink tongue.

Lisa straightened up. "Oh, well, he couldn't have been that hurt in the first place," she said, trying not to laugh at the boy's confusion.

The boy scowled at her. "Whatever," he said. "Come on, Fly. Let's get going."

"Hey! What about the bike? I can't ride it like that," Lisa said with dismay.

"Tough!" The boy grinned.

Lisa was fuming. She opened her
mouth to reply just as a policeman came
around the corner.

The boy groaned. "Oh, great. It's
Mike Sanders. He kicked me off the field
for playing football last week." He threw
a pleading glance at Lisa. "Okay, I *was*
on the wrong side of the road. I couldn't

help it. Some clothes flapping on a line startled Fly and he bolted."

Lisa folded her arms. "So?" she said.

The boy hesitated. "I'll make a deal with you. You keep quiet about me and Fly and I'll fix your bent wheel."

Lisa grinned. "Done! I'm Lisa. Lisa Morgan." She held out her hand. "And this is Flame."

"John Wood," said the boy. He spat in his palm before he shook hands with Lisa, and gave Flame a pat on the head.

The policeman had reached them by now. Mike Sanders had fair curly hair and a pleasant face. He took in the bike with its bent wheel and gave John a stern look. "Hmm. What have you been up to now?"

John looked down at the road and shuffled his feet. "Nothing," he muttered.

Lisa took a step forward. "It's a good thing John came along," she said quickly. "That's my aunt Rose's bike. The wheel bent when I fell over. John's offered to fix it for me."

"Oh really?" Mike Sanders looked surprised. "Good for you, John. That should keep you out of trouble for five minutes." After checking that Lisa wasn't hurt, he went on his way.

"Phew, that was close," said John. He took hold of Fly's reins. "Let's go. I live just over there."

"Don't say 'thanks' for covering for me, or anything?" Lisa said.

John laughed. His blue eyes sparkled. "Okay, I won't!"

Lisa couldn't help laughing back. "Come on, Flame." She lifted him into

the basket and wheeled the bike along
in a wobbly line. John walked ahead,
leading Fly.

"Down here," John said, heading
down a narrow road that branched over
Berry Road.

Lisa paused for a moment as she looked at a large field filled with caravans beyond an open gate.

John turned around. "Well, are you coming or what?"

Flame gave a happy meow. And Lisa pushed him and the wobbly bike through the gate.

Chapter
SIX

The oldest lady Lisa had ever seen
came out of an old-fashioned caravan
with fancy carving and red and yellow
wheels. She waved at John and called for
him to come over.

"That's my great-grandma," John told
Lisa. "Come and meet her."

Lisa lifted Flame out of the basket and
then laid the bike on its side in the grass.
Flame scampered straight up the caravan's
sloping wooden steps and began rubbing
himself against the old lady's long skirts.

"His name is Flame," Lisa told her.

John had tied up Fly before climbing the steps. He gave his gran a kiss on her cheek. "Hi, Gran!"

The old lady's bright eyes crinkled in a smile. "Come on inside and bring your new friends. The kettle's on," she said as she leaned down to pet Flame. "I bet you'd like a bowl of milk, wouldn't you?"

Flame meowed eagerly.

Once inside the tiny living space, Lisa glanced round. Shiny pots and pans hung on hooks above a tiny stove, which made the room very hot. There was a wonderful smell of woodsmoke and lavender polish.

Flame lapped at his milk. He seemed perfectly at home.

John came and sat near his gran.

"Gran, this is Lisa. She's staying with her aunt in the village. Lisa, meet Violet Wood—she's head of our family. Even my dad's afraid of her. But I reckon her bark's a lot worse than her bite!"

Violet gave a gap-toothed grin. "Here! Don't give away all my secrets!" Around her shoulders there was a black fringed shawl with pink roses on it. Big gold hoops glittered in her ears.

"I like your caravan," Lisa said politely as Violet made tea.

"It's my wagon," Violet corrected. "A true gypsy doesn't call their home a caravan."

"Sorry," Lisa said.

Violet looked at her with a gaze as bright and shiny as a robin's. "What you got to be sorry about?"

"Er . . . Nothing," Lisa murmured.

"No reason to say you're sorry then!" Violet crowed.

John chuckled. "Stop teasing, Gran. Lisa's all right. She put a good word in for me with Mike Sanders."

Violet poured strong tea into china cups. "Sanders ain't a bad sort. It's that Robert Higgins you have to watch out for. He's been here again, accusing our men of taking deer. I told him I know everything that goes on around here and there's been no poaching. But he wouldn't have it. He as much as called me a liar to my face!" She sniffed indignantly.

"Who's Robert Higgins?" Lisa asked John.

"Higgins runs the estate for his Lordship," John explained. "That bit of forest at the back of your aunt's cottage is part of it."

"You stay out of his way, John, you hear? He's a nasty piece of work," Violet warned him.

"Yes, Gran." John was serious for a moment and then he turned to Lisa. "Gran used to travel all over the country in this wagon. She's not happy about being here on the official travelers' site."

"I miss the open road too much." Violet's beady eyes brightened. "There was this one time when we was *aitched* up for the night by a river . . ."

"That means camped," John explained, smiling at Lisa.

Violet told them about the old days, when a pony drew her wagon through the country lanes. "All the families would meet up with their relatives at horse fairs. There would be dozens of Woods,

Smiths, Lees, and a hundred other names. Oh, it was grand. In late summer, we'd all travel down to Kent for the hop-picking."

Lisa listened in fascination. A look of contentment settled on Violet's face as she pet Flame's soft coat.

Violet saw Lisa watching closely and said, "Flame's a grand kitten, ain't he?" She closed one eye in a broad wink. "He's just magic."

Lisa's eyes widened in shock. *She knows!* she thought. *Violet knows about Flame!*

"Well, Gran. I've got to get my tools to fix Lisa's bike," John said, apparently not noticing anything. "Thanks for the tea and stories."

"You can bring Lisa and Flame to see

me again." Violet came down the wagon
steps to wave good-bye. She stood with
Lisa as John walked across to a modern,
chrome-trimmed trailer.

"Keep this special one safe," Violet
said softly to Lisa as she pet the top of
Flame's head. "He'll not be with you
long."

Lisa gathered Flame in her embrace. She felt a sharp pang at the thought of not having him around. "I don't want him to leave, ever," she said, her voice quivering.

Violet's eyes sparkled kindly. She patted Lisa's arm. "I know. But his destiny is far from here. When the call comes, he must go. Be thankful that he chose you for his special friend."

Lisa hugged Flame's furry little body close. He purred and licked her chin. She had a lump in her throat. "I am. If I look after him really well, maybe he'll decide to stay here."

A wise but sad look crossed Violet's face. "Maybe," she murmured.

"All done," John said, moving the

bike back and forth. "Good as new!"

He lifted Flame into the basket as Lisa
got on the bike. "Thanks. Aunt Rose
won't notice a thing. Well—bye for
now," she said, and cycled toward the
site gate.

"I'm going fishing tomorrow," John
called after her. "Want to come?"

Lisa had never been fishing, but she thought it might be better than doing nothing at her aunt's cottage. "Okay. Where should we meet?" she shouted.

"Outside the White Hart Inn near the crossroads. Nine A.M.?"

"See you there!" Lisa waved as she turned into the lane.

The sun was low and trees threw long shadows across the road. "That was quite an adventure, wasn't it?" she said to Flame.

Flame meowed in agreement. He curled his front paws over the basket's rim and peered ahead, ears pricked up and fur sparkling.

At the top of the lane, Lisa paused. "Now. Do we go right or left?"

Suddenly a dark-blue van pulled up,

honking loudly. Lisa jumped with fright. The van's broken side-view mirror was only inches away. With a screech of tires, the van sped off.

"Some people have no manners!" Lisa fumed, turning onto Berry Road.

As she rode toward her aunt's cottage, she suddenly felt like she had forgotten something.

Aunt Rose's shopping!

"Oh, no!" she breathed. "Maybe we still have time to go to the shops."

"We are too late." Flame pointed a paw at the red and black VW Beetle, which was coming toward them.

Matilda drew to a halt. Lisa's aunt leaned out of the window, a furious look on her face. "I want a word with you, young lady!" she said.

Lisa's spirits sank. "Uh-oh," she whispered to Flame.

Chapter
SEVEN

Lisa dragged her feet as she followed her aunt into the cottage. There was no way she could avoid a lecture. Flame padded in behind them.

Rose's cheeks were flushed with anger. "You've been gone for hours, Lisa. I've been frantic, driving around looking for you."

"I didn't realize how late it was," Lisa murmured, wondering what all the fuss was about. She was back now, wasn't she?

"You should have come back and

told me where you were going," Rose snapped. "You know that I'm responsible for you while you're here. I thought you were more grown up than this."

Lisa felt an uncomfortable twinge of guilt. "I'm sorry, Aunt Rose. I didn't think." She told her aunt all about almost crashing into John on Fly, then going to the travelers' site and having tea with Violet Wood.

"I'm amazed you weren't hurt when you fell off the bike. And you really should have told me first before going off with someone you've just met! But it sounds like you had a good time," Rose said more calmly. She flopped down on to the sofa and patted the seat next to her.

Lisa sat near her aunt and Flame curled up between them. "John's really nice when you get to know him, Aunt Rose. He fixed the broken wheel." Oops. She hadn't meant to mention that.

But Rose didn't seem to notice. She sighed and put her arm around Lisa's shoulder. "No harm done. So let's forget it. But promise me you'll always tell me where you're going from now on."

"I promise," Lisa said, making a cross-my-heart shape with one finger.

Rose smiled, her good humor restored. She jumped up and went toward the kitchen. "Right, I don't know about you, but I'm starving. Could you bring the shopping inside, please?"

"Um . . ." Lisa's face fell. "Now

I'm really going to get roasted," she
whispered to Flame.

Flame meowed and twitched his
whiskers. Lisa saw that huge silver sparks
were popping in the air around him. The
familiar warmth prickled down her spine.

"Flame! You can't . . . can you?"

She dashed outside to where she had

left the bike leaning against the cottage
wall. The bike's basket was crammed
with food. There was bread, milk,
eggs, and even a gooey, homemade
chocolate cake.

"Oh, you star!" Lisa swept Flame up
in a huge hug. She kissed his pink nose.
"You've just saved my life!"

Flame widened his eyes. He stopped in mid-purr. "Are you in danger, Lisa?"

"No. It's just something you say." Lisa giggled.

Rose threw up her hands with delight when she saw the cake. "That's my favorite!"

"My treat," Lisa said, biting back a huge grin. She would have loved to say Flame chose it!

That evening after dinner, Lisa washed the dishes without a second thought. She smiled to herself; she must be getting used to life in the countryside! Afterward, she made a cup of coffee for her aunt and took it into the living room. Flame was curled up asleep on his blanket.

"Thanks. I could get used to this," Rose joked. "So, what did you think of Violet Wood?"

"She's great. I loved her cara— wagon," Lisa corrected herself. "It was really small inside, but with a wood stove and bed and everything. Violet told us some stories about her traveling days."

"I expect it was a wonderful life," Rose said. "It's a shame that some things have to change so much. Violet rules the Wood family with a rod of iron—even the men! She really must have taken to you. I've never heard of anyone from the village being invited to have tea with her."

"Violet loved Flame, too," Lisa said. "But not as much as I do." She glanced at the sleeping kitten, a warm glow filling her chest.

Rose smiled. "The Woods seem like a really nice, friendly family."

Lisa was glad her aunt approved of John Wood and his family. "Do you know Mr. Higgins? Violet didn't seem to think much of him."

Rose snorted. "Robert Higgins isn't a nice man. You'd think twice about getting on his wrong side. He's jumped

81

to the conclusion that the travelers have been poaching deer."

"Violet said she told Mr. Higgins that she was sure none of their men had been poaching deer, but he didn't believe her," Lisa told her aunt. If Violet didn't think any of the Wood family had poached deer, then neither did Lisa.

She jumped up. "I'll go and feed the animals." She tickled Flame gently to wake him up. "Are you coming, Flame?"

Flame yawned and stretched. He purred eagerly and jumped down.

Rose stood up, too. "Thanks, love. I've still got this patchwork quilt to finish. I lost a bit of time going off to look for someone who was late coming home," she said with a twinkle in her eye.

In the barn, Lisa filled food dishes and water bottles and replaced soiled bedding. As she fed chopped carrots to the rabbits and guinea pigs, a thought came to her.

"Where did that magic food come from?" she asked Flame.

"I took it from the shop. Like you wanted," Flame said. He frowned. "Did I do something wrong?"

"No. But I'd better go and pay for it. I still have the shopping money in my pocket. We'll ride over there and deliver it and I'll scribble a note to explain things." Lisa grabbed her shoulder bag. "Come on, Flame. Jump in. We'll only be a few minutes. There's no need to tell Aunt Rose."

Lisa and Flame hurried across the green toward the line of shops. She pushed the envelope through the village store's mailbox.

"Job done," she said happily, patting Flame's soft fur. "I really love having you here with me."

"I like it, too," Flame purred contentedly from the opening of her shoulder bag.

The first stars glinted in the violet sky. A smudge of fading peach light just showed above the church spire.

"It's getting dark," Lisa said worriedly. "We'd better get back before Aunt Rose finds out or she'll ground me for the rest of the vacation!"

She started jogging toward the cottage. There was a sign beside a trail she hadn't noticed before. It read "To Lower Berry Road."

"It must be a shortcut. We'll go that way!"

On one side of the trail there were open fields. Thick woods that were part of the estate Robert Higgins looked after stretched away on the other side.

Lisa had been walking for about five minutes when there was a loud bang.

"Oh!" she gasped, nearly jumping out of her skin. "What was that?"

Flame reared up out of the shoulder bag. The fur along his back stood on end. "Danger!" he hissed.

Lisa's breath came faster. She saw beams of light moving through the trees. There were shouts and men moving toward her. More bangs broke the silence.

"They sound like gunshots," Lisa said

shakily. "Come on, Flame. We're getting out of here!"

She clutched the shoulder bag in her arms so that she could run faster without jostling Flame about. She had taken a couple of steps when a dark-blue van drove up. It screeched to a halt, blocking Lisa's way. Lisa spotted the broken side-view mirror.

"It's that van again!" she whispered to Flame.

The driver leaned out of the side window. He shouted to a man coming out of the trees. "Who's that kid? Go and find out!"

Icy fear curdled Lisa's stomach. She couldn't move.

Chapter
EIGHT

A warm tingle spread over Lisa. She felt the sparks crackling in Flame's fur beneath her hand.

"You are safe," Flame assured her softly.

A moment later, a man dashed up to where Lisa was standing. He stared straight at her. "What kid? There's no one here," the man shouted to the van driver.

Lisa gave a shudder of relief. Flame had made her invisible!

"We must go now," urged Flame.

Lisa didn't need telling twice. She ran past the van, where the driver was still frowning in confusion.

Five minutes later she emerged onto Berry Road. She could see her aunt's cottage. Running the last few feet, she slipped into the back garden and crept into the kitchen.

The sound of her aunt's sewing machine came from her workroom. Lisa stuck her head around the door. "I'm going to my room now, Aunt Rose. I want to read for a while."

Rose looked up with a smile. "Okay, love. Thanks for seeing to the animals. I'll look in on you before I go to bed."

Lisa heaved a sigh of relief as she climbed the stairs. She had only just about stopped trembling. What had those

men in the woods been doing? Maybe
they were shooting crows or rabbits.
They had seemed really angry at being
disturbed.

Thank goodness for Flame. Once
again he had saved her!

"Have you made any plans for today?" Rose asked the following morning. Sunshine set rainbow patterns dancing from the crystal hanging in the window.

Lisa told her she was meeting John. "We're going fishing."

"Are you taking Flame with you?" asked Rose.

"You bet!" Lisa said. She wouldn't dream of leaving him behind. Especially after the way Flame had saved her last night.

Flame wound himself around her legs affectionately.

Rose reached down to pet him. "Well, have fun, you two. Be back in plenty of time for supper, okay?"

"Definitely," Lisa promised. "Come on, Flame, jump in." Looping her bag onto her shoulder, she set out for the White Hart.

John and Fly were already waiting when Lisa and Flame arrived. "The river's this way," John said. They went past the green to a line of silvery willow trees.

The river gleamed through the swaying branches. John led the way down a grassy bank. "Our family's got special permission to fish here. Dad helps clear waterweed away in spring."

Flame stretched out in the grass and closed his eyes, purring contentedly. Fly, who was cropping the sweet grass, swung his head around and gave Flame a friendly snort.

"I can't get over how much Fly likes

that kitten," said John, setting out his fishing things.

Lisa smiled. "Flame's not just any old kitten. He's really special."

John passed Lisa a fishing rod and a small, battered can. "You can use my spare rod. Do you think you can bait it yourself?"

"Sure! How hard can it be?" Lisa opened the can. It was full of little, squirming white bodies. "Ugh! Maggots!" she gasped.

John grinned. "You nearly dropped the whole thing! What did you think was in there, bread crumbs?"

"Something like that!" Lisa admitted, blushing. "I don't think I can hook one of these on."

"Give them to me. It's easy. I'll do it

for you." John gave her the baited rod
and showed Lisa how to cast the line
into the river. Lisa soon had the hang
of it and they settled down to wait for a
bite.

The scent of warm grass drifted on

the river breeze. A duck picked her way through the reeds.

"You've got a bite!" John suddenly declared. He reeled in the fish and slipped it into a net in the water. "There you go. One fat brown trout."

"This is fun!" Lisa said. She felt proud of catching her very first fish.

John beamed at her. "You're not bad company for a girl *and* a townie!"

"Watch it! You . . . you road rogue!" Lisa laughed.

"Road . . . what?" John asked as he fell over laughing.

"Hello there! Caught anything yet?" called a voice. Mike Sanders came along the river path, a smile on his pleasant face.

"Not again," John groaned, but he nodded politely.

Mike Sanders peered into the net. "That's a fine dinner for someone."

"Yeah, it's Lisa's first-ever fish," John said.

Mike Sanders smiled at Lisa. "Beginner's luck, eh?" His face suddenly turned more serious. "Now, I don't suppose you've

heard anything about a couple of deer that were killed last night, John?" he asked.

John shook his head. "Why ask me?"

"Because I reckon you've got a level head on your shoulders. You'd know where to come if you got wind of anyone poaching around here, wouldn't you?" Sanders said.

John shrugged. "I might. But I don't know anything."

"Where were they killed?" Lisa asked.

"In the woods near Lower Berry Road," Sanders told her. "Near where your aunt Rose lives." He gave John a friendly pat on the back. "Well—keep your eyes peeled." He looked back before continuing down the river path and called over his shoulder, "Hope the fish keep biting."

Lisa stared after him, her thoughts whirling as she remembered the shots in the woods last night and the men with flashlights among the trees. Then there was the blue van, which she had seen twice now.

She had been tempted to tell Mike Sanders her suspicions, but she didn't have any proof. And she'd have to explain what she'd been doing out near the woods at night. That meant risking getting into trouble again with Aunt Rose.

Were those men the deer poachers? She pressed her lips together in determination. She and Flame were going to find out.

Chapter
NINE

Lisa stared out of the cottage window as drops streamed down the glass. It had been raining all afternoon. Aunt Rose was at the village hall running a workshop on making patchwork quilts. Lisa felt restless.

Flame jumped on to the windowsill. He batted at the glass, trying to catch the raindrops. Lisa laughed and dangled a piece of wool for him to catch. "You want to go out, too, don't you? I hope it stops raining before tonight."

Flame nodded and wrinkled his little

pink nose. "I do not like wet fur."

Lisa planned to wait until dark and then go back up to the woods and have a good look around.

Just then she heard a knock at the kitchen door. It was John on Fly.

Lisa took one look at him. "What's wrong?" she gasped.

John was soaked to the skin. His hair was plastered flat and his face looked pale and angry. "It's my dad. He's been taken to the police station. They think he's been poaching deer," John told her as he tethered Fly to the back porch. He looked like he might burst into tears.

"Oh, that's awful. I'm really sorry," Lisa sympathized. She grabbed a towel so John could dry himself.

John's shoulders slumped as he

sank into a kitchen chair. "It's Robert Higgins's doing. I know it is. But I don't get it. What's he got against my dad? He's never done anything to him."

Lisa bit her lip, wishing she could think of some way to help. She got him a piece of the delicious chocolate cake. "Here you are."

He cheered up a bit as he ate. "Gran's furious, but she's worried, too. If only there was something I could do."

"Maybe there is," Lisa said on impulse.

She told John about the gunfire and the men she'd seen in the woods. "And I've seen that blue van twice. I know it was the same one because of the broken side-view mirror."

John jumped to his feet and paced

around the kitchen. "It must have been the poachers! Deer are big animals. You'd need a van to take them away. Maybe we should go and tell Mike Sanders."

"I thought of that already. But we don't have any proof. Shouldn't we

wait until we're sure about this?" Lisa reasoned.

John gnawed at his lip. "You're right. And if the police start going around asking tons of questions, the poachers will go into hiding. That leaves my dad as the chief suspect. But how do we get proof?"

"I've got an idea . . ." Lisa began telling him about her plan to go to the woods after dark.

John listened in silence, then a wide grin spread across his face. "What time do we meet?"

"We?" Lisa grinned back. "I hoped you might say that!"

"You don't think I'd let you have all the fun, do you?" John said. He got up and went toward the garden to untie Fly.

Lisa was relieved. It had been really scary up in those dark woods.

"All right," she said. "I'll meet you at midnight on the back path to the woods. Don't do anything before I get there, okay?"

"Who, me?" John flashed her one of his grins. He jumped up onto Fly's back and urged the pony forward. "See you tonight," he called over his shoulder.

The bedroom was dark except for the digital display of her bedside clock. Lisa jolted awake. Flame was licking her chin. His whiskers tickled her nose.

"Thanks for waking me!" She yawned and rubbed her eyes.

"You are welcome," Flame purred, his fur twinkling in the darkness.

It was a quarter to midnight. No time to waste. Lisa was fully clothed beneath the covers. Reaching for her bag and a disposable camera, she and Flame crept downstairs and out of the house.

The moon sailed overhead, as bright as a beacon. Lisa's eyes soon adjusted as she made her way to the woods. Flame trotted beside her. With his cat night-sight he moved as easily as in daylight.

"This is the path," Lisa whispered, pointing ahead. "But look! The blue van's parked near those bushes."

Lisa's heart pounded as she and Flame crept forward. She scanned the path and clusters of trees, looking for John. But there was no sign of him.

Flame pricked up his ears. "There are men in these woods."

A moment later, Lisa heard voices shouting. "Get him! He knows who we are!"

Shadowy shapes crashed through the trees. Someone shoved branches aside and rushed toward Lisa, gasping for breath. For an instant a slim, scared figure was caught in a beam of the flashlight.

Lisa's eyes opened wide with shock. "It's John!"

Chapter
TEN

Almost immediately Lisa felt the familiar tingly warmth down her spine. Silver sparks crackled in Flame's fur and his whiskers glittered in the dark.

"No one can see you, Lisa," Flame explained softly. He hung back, melting into the deep shadows. "Save John."

Lisa let out a sigh of relief. Flame had made her invisible again!

John stumbled out of a thicket right beside her. Leaning against a big oak, he doubled over, clutching a stitch in his side. Lisa could hear the men coming

closer. They would catch John at any
moment. She had to distract them
somehow.

Lisa started to run, her heart
pounding. Her whole body began to
tingle. A rush of heat swept through her.
She felt her muscles bunch as she made
a huge leap forward—and bounded along

on all fours. Strong, tireless legs carried her on. Her hands and feet had become spread pads, which gripped the leaf litter with sharp claws.

She was a huge cat! A huge *invisible* cat!

Night smells flowed over her. The forest came alive. She could see every leaf and blade of grass and hear every tiny movement. The men seemed to move in slow motion. Their breath sounded like rushing water and their footsteps were as loud as drumbeats.

Lisa rushed up behind the first man and slammed into the back of his legs. He yelled with fright as his knees buckled. In a swift movement, Lisa changed direction and launched herself at another man.

"Oof!" The second man fell sideways.

"Grrr!" Lisa growled with triumph.

She tripped up the third man, who fell
over in a jumble of arms and legs.

The three men picked themselves up.
They looked around nervously. "There's

something weird in here!" one said.

Lisa grinned. She crept up close behind them and opened her mouth wide. "Grrr-owl!!" she roared.

"What's that?"

"I don't know, but I'm out of here!" one of them cried. "Get back to the van!"

Lisa knew that John was safe for the moment. Time to get the evidence they needed.

She bounded swiftly toward the parked van and reached it ahead of the men. The back door was ajar. Her cat senses caught the smell of death. Two deer lay in the back of the van. Lisa jumped inside, already fumbling for her camera. Her fingers closed around it.

Fingers? She wasn't a cat anymore!

Flame's spell must have worn off. Did that mean that the men could see her now?

There was no time to think. Aiming the camera, she took a photo of the dead deer. Suddenly, the back door was wrenched open behind her. But Lisa was ready. She stuck the camera in the men's faces. *Flash! Flash!* She took their photos.

"Wassat?" one yelled, covering his face with his hand.

"I can't see. I'm blinded," moaned another, hopping around and bumping into his friends.

Lisa leaped out and dashed behind a tree. Moments later, the engine fired up and the van sped off up the road.

Lisa leaned against the tree and gave a nervous shaky laugh. Wow! That was close. She loved being a cat! She couldn't wait to talk to Flame all about it.

She glanced around for him. Where was he? He usually kept close beside her. As she made her way back toward the road, she called softly, "Flame. Where are you?"

"I am here," came a tiny whimper. Flame crawled out from beneath some ferns. His eyes were wide with alarm.

Lisa picked him up. "Oh, you're trembling." She pet his head and gave him a cuddle. "Don't be scared for me. Your magic was amazing! Those horrible men have left."

But Flame nestled closer, his tiny heart beating fast. Lisa felt a stir of unease as he gave another little whimper.

Just then John ran up to her. "Lisa?

Where have you been? You missed all the fun!" he panted. "I know who the poachers are!"

Lisa gently tucked Flame into her shoulder bag. He would be warm and safe in there. "Did you get a good look at them?" she asked.

John's face was white, except for a smudge of dirt on his cheek. He nodded. "Two of them are friends of Higgins's! He must be in on it. No wonder he's trying to blame my dad. They tried to catch me, but I lost them in the woods."

"I'm just glad you're safe," Lisa said, relieved that they were both okay.

John frowned. "I might be safe, but I still don't have any proof. It's my word against theirs."

Lisa felt in her pocket for the camera.

She imagined the look on John's face when he found out she had taken photos. But her fingers closed on nothing but empty space.

Oh, no! The camera wasn't there. She must have dropped it in the woods!

"Photos? How did you get photos? You just got here!" John frowned at Lisa in puzzlement when she had explained.

Lisa thought quickly. She couldn't let John know about Flame's magic. "I saw the blue van on my way to meet you. No one was around. So I risked taking some photos. But I nearly got caught when they came back!"

John looked impressed. He whistled through his teeth. "Those photos will prove my dad had nothing to do with poaching deer. We really need to find that camera. I'll look over where the van was parked."

"Okay. I'll look over here." Lisa went a little way into the woods. Opening her shoulder bag, she whispered to Flame, "Can you help me find the camera, please? I have to be getting back. Aunt Rose will be furious if she finds out I've sneaked out here at this time of night!"

Flame was curled into a tight ball in one corner. He lifted his head and gazed at her with fearful eyes. "I must hide. My enemies are close. Uncle Ebony's spies are almost here," he meowed.

"Oh, no!" Lisa's chest constricted. No wonder Flame was acting strangely. He was in terrible danger.

Chapter
ELEVEN

"You have to leave here, Flame!
Now!" Lisa urged in a shaky voice. Tears
pricked her eyes. The thought of her
friend leaving was heartbreaking. But
Flame's life was in danger and she knew
he must go.

Flame shook his head. His eyes were
dull and his fur was flat. "I am too weak.
I need strong magic to find a new place
to hide soon. But not now," he told her
in a small voice.

Lisa gulped back tears. She was secretly
relieved that they could be together a

little longer, but she was still worried for his safety. She pet his little velvety ears. "Please be careful, Flame. I couldn't bear it if they found you."

Turning his head, Flame touched the tip of Lisa's index finger with his nose. "You must find the camera."

Lisa's finger felt warm and tingly and the end began glowing softly. She understood what she must do.

Flame's head drooped and he curled back into a tight ball. Lisa saw with dismay that only two or three little silver sparkles glinted in his fur.

There was no time to waste. Lisa clutched her shoulder bag to her side and began searching for the camera, using her glowing finger as a guide. She pushed leaf mold aside and poked under fallen

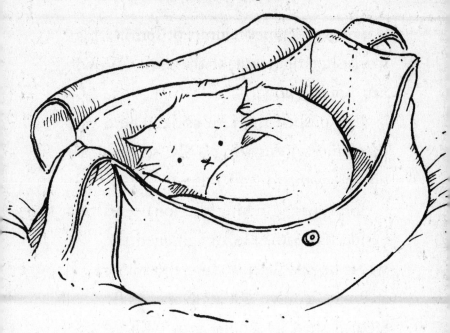

twigs. As she moved toward a tuft of grass, her finger stopped glowing. "I must be getting cold."

She turned back toward a group of birch trees and her finger glowed faintly. "Now I'm getting hotter."

She kept searching, watching for her magic finger to give her clues. As she

stood over a thick clump of ferns, a big
spark shot right out of the end. "Wow!
I'm boiling now!"

Lisa pushed the fern aside. There was
the camera. "Amazing!" She scooped it
up and went to find John.

John was searching the long grass
beside the path. He straightened up
when he saw Lisa waving the camera
at him. "You've got it? Great!" His
teeth flashed in a huge grin. "I'll get the
photos developed first thing tomorrow
morning. Gran will come with me to see
Mike Sanders. I would like to see anyone
argue with her, once they see the photos!
Thanks a million, Lisa."

Lisa blushed. "Glad we could help."

"We?" John said, looking a little
confused.

"Me and Flame," Lisa said.

"Oh, yeah!" John chuckled. "Thanks, Flame. You'd better go now. Your aunt will skin me alive if she finds you out here with me!"

Lisa smiled and waved good-bye as she hurried back to her aunt's cottage.

She didn't see the long black shadows prowling through the trees. Two large black cats appeared for an instant. One of them lifted its head, scenting the air before they both disappeared.

There came a faint echo of a powerful voice. "The prince is near. We are close . . ."

Lisa crept in the back door and up through the darkened cottage.

"Phew, made it," she breathed, closing

her bedroom door behind her.

Now that the excitement was over, she felt really tired. She undressed and crawled into bed. Flame jumped up and settled down beside her. He reached forward and touched her chin gently with the tip of his cold, pink nose.

"You are a good friend, Lisa," he said with a rumbling purr. "I will never forget you."

A hard ball of misery lodged in her chest and her eyes filled with tears, but she swallowed them bravely. "Me too. I've loved having you here, Flame. But I know you have to leave soon."

"Soon," Flame agreed sadly and snuggled up under her chin.

Moments later, Lisa fell deeply asleep.

The next day, Lisa was in the barn.
She was filling dishes with scoops of
pet food and trying not to think about
Flame leaving. She knew she should be
feeling happier—she had heard from her
aunt earlier that day that Higgins and his
friends had been arrested. But she was
just so sad at the thought of losing Flame.
Right then he was sitting on the sack of
food where she had first discovered him,
his eyes watchful and intent. He kept
lifting his head, testing the air for his
enemies' scent.

Lisa had her arms full of hay when she
heard her aunt calling. "Lisa! You've got
visitors!"

She looked up to see her aunt and
two other people coming into the barn.

"Mom! Dad!" she cried with delight

as she ran toward them and threw herself into their arms. "What are you doing here?"

Mrs. Morgan laughed. "We missed you. So we came back early. Rose has asked us to stop by for a few days before we all go back to London." She turned to her sister with a smile.

"You don't mind, do you, love?" asked Mr. Morgan, looking a bit worried. "I know you've probably been really bored here in the country."

Lisa realized that she had enjoyed herself far more than she ever thought possible. And this was mainly due to Flame. She was about to reply that she'd had a fantastic time when she noticed a flash of light from near the sack of food.

"Why don't you go into the kitchen?"

she said hurriedly. "I'll finish feeding the animals, then I'll come, too."

Rose led Lisa's parents out of the barn. "Let's leave Lisa to it. She always insists on getting her chores finished by herself. She's been a great help to me."

"Really? That doesn't sound like the grumpy girl we dropped off at the train station last week!" Lisa's dad said with surprise.

"She certainly looks a lot happier than I expected!" said her mom, looking slightly amazed. "See you in a minute," she called over her shoulder.

As soon as they had left, Lisa spun around. She ran toward the back of the barn and stopped in her tracks, stunned by what she saw.

An enormous young white lion with

glowing emerald eyes stood there. His fur glittered and sparkled and his whiskers glowed with light. Prince Flame was no longer disguised as a fluffy orange kitten. Beside him stood an older-looking gray lion, a calm expression on his wise face.

As Lisa watched, silver sparks filled the air. The two lions began to fade. Prince Flame lifted his paw in a final wave. His mouth curved in a gentle smile.

"Be well. Be strong, Lisa," he said in a deep growling purr.

Then he was gone.

Lisa stood there, a wave of deep sadness flowing over her. She wondered where Flame would go now to hide. Would he ever be safe from his uncle's spies? Would he one day rule his strange, magical land?

"Good-bye, Prince Flame," Lisa whispered. "Take care. Stay safe. I'll never forget you."

She stood there for a moment longer, thinking of the wonderful adventure she and Flame had shared. Even though her heart was aching, she knew she wouldn't have changed a single moment.

At last, she took a deep trembling breath. Her parents were waiting for her. She knew she would never tell them or anyone else about Flame. He would always be her very own magical secret. But there was still so much more to tell them. And she couldn't wait for them to meet John and Fly.

About the Author

Sue Bentley's books for children often include animals or fairies. She lives in Northampton and enjoys reading, going to the cinema, and sitting and watching the frogs and newts in her garden pond. If she hadn't been a writer she would probably have been a skydiver or a brain surgeon. The main reason she writes is that she can drink pots and pots of tea while she's typing. She has met and owned many cats and each one has brought a special sort of magic to her life.